FE 1 7

It's Time

Story Time

Bonnie Phelps

illustrated by
Aurora Aguilera

PowerKiDS
press.

New York

Published in 2017 by The Rosen Publishing Group, Inc.
29 East 21st Street, New York, NY 10010

First Edition

Managing Editor: Nathalie Beullens-Maoui
Editor: Caitie McAneney
Book Design: Michael Flynn
Illustrator: Aurora Aguilera

Cataloging-in-Publication Data

Names: Phelps, Bonnie.
Title: Story time / Bonnie Phelps.
Description: New York : Powerkids Press, 2016. | Series: It's time | Includes index.
Identifiers: ISBN 9781508152156 (pbk.) | ISBN 9781508152170 (library bound) | ISBN 9781508152163 (6 pack)
Subjects: LCSH: Storytelling–Juvenile literature.
Classification: LCC GR74.P54 2016 | DDC 808.5′43 –dc23

Manufactured in the United States of America

CPSIA Compliance Information: Batch #BS16PK: For Further Information contact Rosen Publishing, New York, New York at 1-800-237-9932

Contents

My grandma asks me to
pick out a book.

It's story time!

Grandma loves to read.
She has hundreds of books!

I choose a book about animals
in the forest.

There's a bear on
the cover!

Grandma says books can
teach us a lot.

I learn about deer and snakes.

Next, I pick a storybook.

It's about a
funny rabbit.

13

I like when Grandma
reads to me.

She uses different voices for different characters.

I like to look at pictures in books.

Pictures make the story come alive!

Grandma tells me a story.

18

It's about a brave princess.

I make up a story about a scared owl.

Making up stories is fun!

I love story time!

Every book has a story to tell.

Words to Know

bear

rabbit

snakes

Index

24